A Pirate's Twelve Days of Christmas

by **Philip Yates**

illustrated by **Sebastià Serra**

STERLING CHILDREN'S BOOKS

New York

'Twas on the eve of Christmastide our ship sailed in the night
across the dark and briny deep beneath the stars so bright.

"Ahoy, me mates!" the Cap'n roared. "'Tis time to plunder wrecks—
except fer you, me cabin boy—ye'll stay an' swab the decks!"

I told him it was Christmastide. "Arrrgh-humbug!" Cap'n barked.
"That holiday's fer landlubbers! Ye'll stay put on the *Sark*!"

That night I dreamed of Christmas trees a-sparklin' 'neath the moon
an' jolly ol' Sir Peggedy with sacks full of doubloons.

But when I woke I saw a sight: "What's this upon our ship?
AVAST!" I cried, an' danced a jig. A song burst from me lips:

On the first day of Christmas,
a gift was sent to me:

a parrot in a palm tree!

On the second day of Christmas,
a gift was sent to me:

2 cutlasses

an' a parrot in a palm tree.

On the third day of Christmas,
a gift was sent to me:

3 black cats

2 cutlasses, an' a parrot in a palm tree.

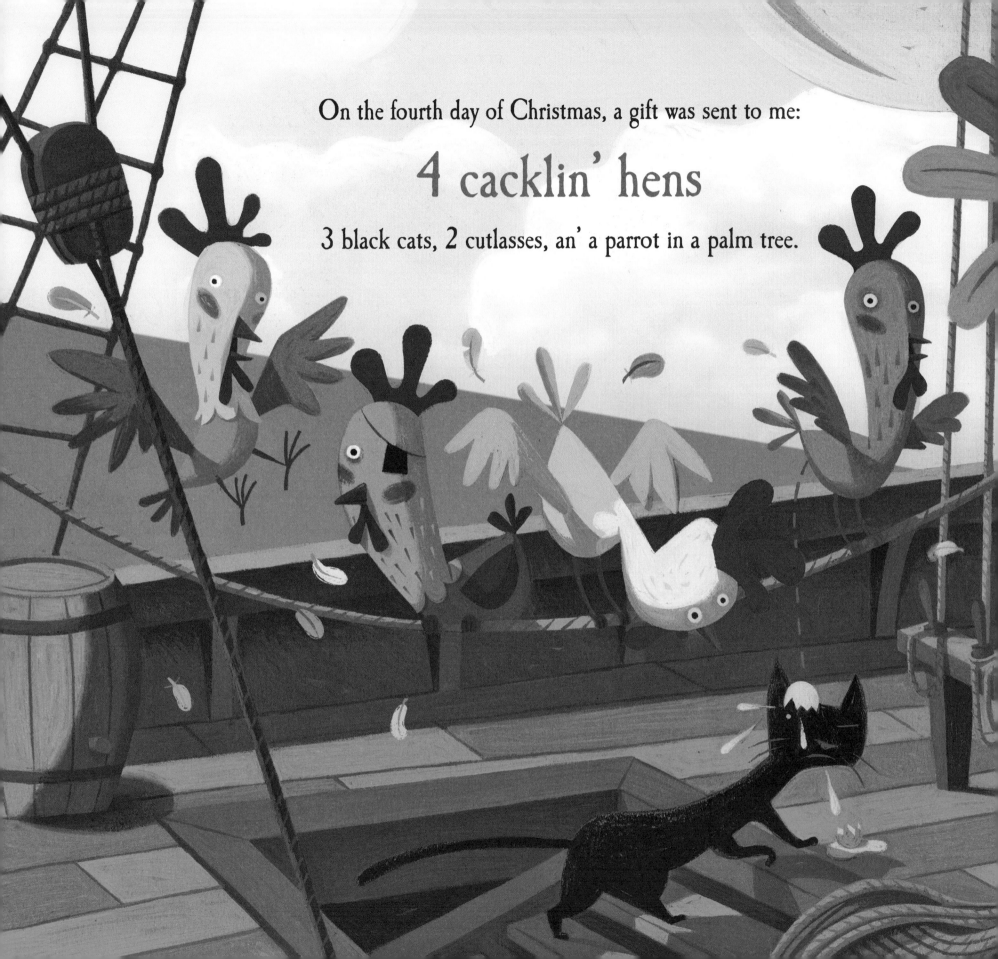

On the fourth day of Christmas, a gift was sent to me:

4 cacklin' hens

3 black cats, 2 cutlasses, an' a parrot in a palm tree.

On the fifth day of Christmas, a gift was sent to me:

5 chests of gold!

4 cacklin' hens, 3 black cats, 2 cutlasses,
an' a parrot in a palm tree.

On the sixth day of Christmas,
a gift was sent to me:

6 Jolly Rogers

5 chests of gold, 4 cacklin' hens,
3 black cats, 2 cutlasses,
an' a parrot in a palm tree.

On the seventh day of Christmas,
a gift was sent to me:

7 monkeys swingin'

6 Jolly Rogers, 5 chests of gold, 4 cacklin' hens,
3 black cats, 2 cutlasses, an' a parrot in a palm tree.

On the eighth day of Christmas, a gift was sent to me:

8 dolphins swimmin'

7 monkeys swingin', 6 Jolly Rogers, 5 chests of gold,
4 cacklin' hens, 3 black cats, 2 cutlasses, an' a parrot in a palm tree.

On the ninth day of Christmas, a gift was sent to me:

9 mermaids singin'

8 dolphins swimmin', 7 monkeys swingin',
6 Jolly Rogers, 5 chests of gold, 4 cacklin' hens,
3 black cats, 2 cutlasses,
an' a parrot in a palm tree.

On the tenth day of Christmas, a gift was sent to me:

10 sloops a-sailin'

9 mermaids singin', 8 dolphins swimmin',
7 monkeys swingin', 6 Jolly Rogers,
5 chests of gold, 4 cacklin' hens, 3 black cats,
2 cutlasses, an' a parrot in a palm tree.

On the eleventh day of Christmas, a gift was sent to me:

11 swallows swoopin'

10 sloops a-sailin', 9 mermaids singin', 8 dolphins swimmin',
7 monkeys swingin', 6 Jolly Rogers, 5 chests of gold,
4 cacklin' hens, 3 black cats, 2 cutlasses, an' a parrot in a palm tree.

On the twelfth day of Christmas,
a gift was sent to me:

12 pirates cheerin'

11 swallows swoopin', 10 sloops a-sailin', 9 mermaids singin',
8 dolphins swimmin', 7 monkeys swingin', 6 Jolly Rogers,
5 chests of gold, 4 cacklin' hens,
3 black cats, 2 cutlasses,
an' a parrot in a palm tree.

"SURPRISE!" me buckos shouted. The Cap'n winked at me.
"Merry Christmas, laddie boy—we sent those gifts to ye."

"HOORAY!"

The Cap'n cried, "'Tis time fer bed. Avast! Anchors aweigh!
Fer jolly ol' Sir Peggedy will soon be on his sleigh!"
I thanked me hearties, one an' all, for every gift they'd sent,
then sang a little sleepy song, an' this is how it went:

On the last night of Christmas, me mateys gave to me:

12 pirates snorin', 11 swallows roostin', 10 sloops a-driftin',
9 mermaids dreamin', 8 dolphins drowsin', 7 monkeys dozin',
6 flags a-fallin', 5 beds of gold, 4 nestin' hens,
3 cat naps, 2 sleepin' swords . . .

. . . an' a parrot a-snoozin' with me.

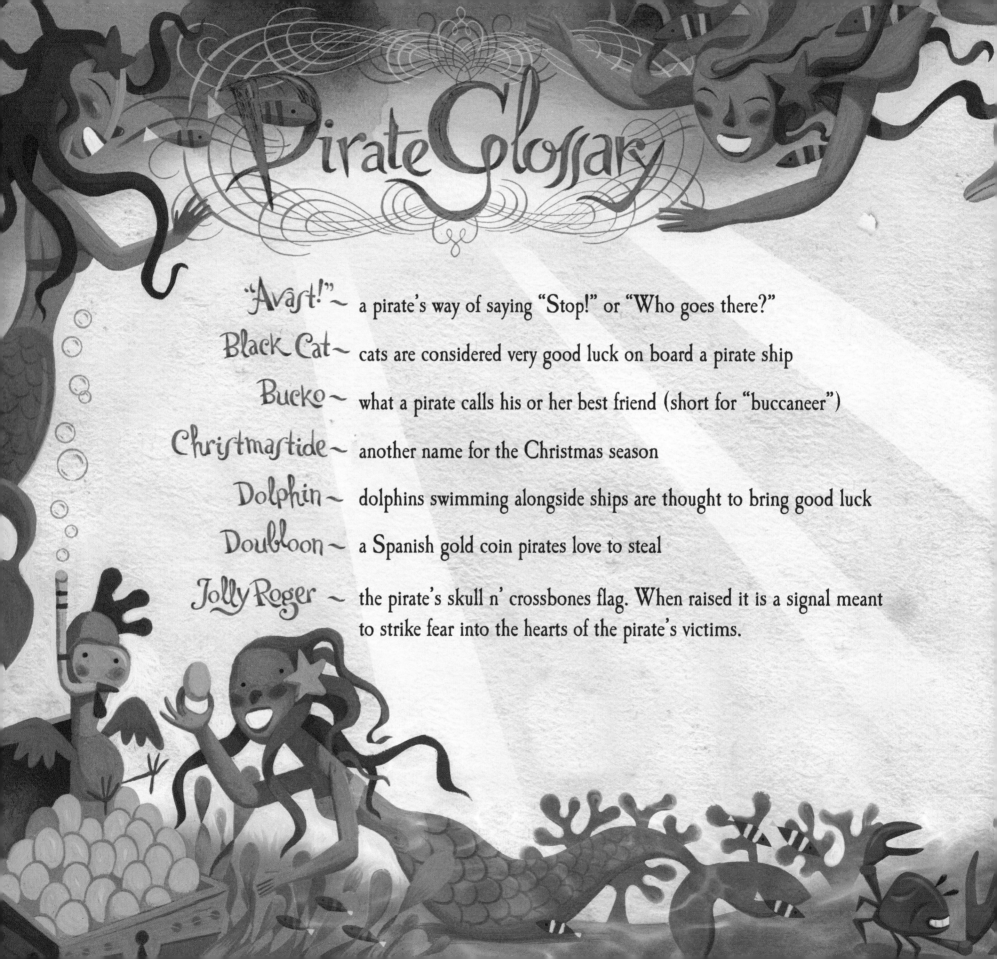

Pirate Glossary

"Avast!" ~ a pirate's way of saying "Stop!" or "Who goes there?"

Black Cat ~ cats are considered very good luck on board a pirate ship

Bucko ~ what a pirate calls his or her best friend (short for "buccaneer")

Christmastide ~ another name for the Christmas season

Dolphin ~ dolphins swimming alongside ships are thought to bring good luck

Doubloon ~ a Spanish gold coin pirates love to steal

Jolly Roger ~ the pirate's skull n' crossbones flag. When raised it is a signal meant to strike fear into the hearts of the pirate's victims.

Landlubber ~ "land lover," someone who prefers to stay on land

Mateys and Hearties ~ a pirate's shipmates

Plunder ~ what a pirate does when robbing loot from other ships

Sark ~ short for the *Black Sark*, the name of the ship in this book. One of the most famous
pirate ships in history was called the *Cutty Sark*, which was a sailing ship with three masts.

Sloop ~ a small sailboat with a single mast, similar to a dinghy

Swallow ~ spotting a swallow means that land is near and smooth sailing is ahead

Thar ~ sometimes used for "there" and sometimes for "their"

To Maria:
Twelve days of Christmas just fer you—but wait—I have it wrong—
Thar's somethin' missin', lassie dear, from this cheery song.
I love you not fer just twelve days, fer how could I survive?
Twelve days of Christmas? Arrgh-humbug! Three hundred sixty five!
Love, P.Y.

To Judy Sue, April, Talia, and Mike of Studio Goodwin Sturges—thank you for sailing with me
on the seas of literature, and providing such high spirits and good company along the way.
—S.S.

STERLING CHILDREN'S BOOKS
New York
An Imprint of Sterling Publishing
387 Park Avenue South
New York, NY 10016

STERLING CHILDREN'S BOOKS and the distinctive Sterling Children's Books logo are trademarks of Sterling Publishing Co., Inc.

Text © 2012 Philip Yates
Illustrations © 2012 Sebastià Serra
The illustrations in this book were created using pencil and ink on parchment paper and then digitally colored. The display lettering was created by Sebastià Serra.
Designed by Elizabeth Phillips

ISBN 978-1-4027-9225-0

LIBRARY OF CONGRESS CATALOGING-IN-PUBLICATION DATA

Yates, Philip.
A pirate's twelve days of Christmas / by Philip Yates ; [illustrations, Sebastia Serra].
p. cm.
ISBN 978-1-4027-9225-0 (hardback)
1. Santa Claus—Juvenile poetry. 2. Pirates—Juvenile poetry. 3. Children's poetry, American. 4. Christmas poetry. I. Serra, Sebastia, 1966- II. Title.
PS3575.A825P57 2012
811'.54—dc2

2012011394

Distributed in Canada by Sterling Publishing
c/o Canadian Manda Group, 165 Dufferin Street
Toronto, Ontario, Canada M6K 3H6
Distributed in the United Kingdom by GMC Distribution Services
Castle Place, 166 High Street, Lewes, East Sussex, England BN7 1XU
Distributed in Australia by Capricorn Link (Australia) Pty. Ltd.
P.O. Box 704, Windsor, NSW 2756, Australia

For information about custom editions, special sales, and premium and corporate purchases, please contact Sterling Special Sales at 800-805-5489 or specialsales@sterlingpublishing.com.

Printed in China
Lot #:
2 4 6 8 10 9 7 5 3 1
07/12

www.sterlingpublishing.com/kids

Merry Christmas, me buckos!